The Dragon's Keeper

T. L. Riffey

Copyright © 2021 T. L. Riffey
All cover art copyright © 2021 T. L. Riffey
All Rights Reserved

This is a work of fiction. Names, places, characters and incidents are either the product of the author's imagination or are used fictitiously, and any resemblance to any actual persons, living or dead, businesses, organizations, events or locales is entirely coincidental.

No part of this book may be reproduced or transmitted in any form or by any means, electronic or mechanical, including photocopying, recording, or by any information storage and retrieval system, without permission in writing from the author.

Publishing Coordinator – Sharon Kizziah-Holmes

Paperback-Press
an imprint of A & S Publishing
A & S Holmes, Inc.

ISBN -13: 978-1-956806-21-2

For dragon-lovers
May you find your own dragon shrine

PROLOGUE

The cloaked riders halted.

Around them were stone ruins barely seen through the blowing sand. A tall facade loomed darkly in front of them and a smaller one reared to their right.

Rissa slid off the back of her master's horse and came around to hold the beast as her master himself dismounted. She could just hear the others getting off their horses over the sound of the small sandstorm. The storm had stirred up an hour ago and was already winding down. There had been several of these little dusters during their journey here and they no longer caused her anxiety. She was not a desert child. Forests were more her element.

Her master took his horse's reins, then pushed

her away. "See to the boy," he told her harshly.

She immediately headed past him. Two cloaked figures were standing beside a horse behind her master's. The second one was smaller and the taller shoved the shorter one at her. She grabbed his arm to keep him from falling, then she moved both of them away from the men. They would be setting up camp with the supplies on the ponies they had brought with them. Most of the time she would be helping the other slaves with the camp, but she was the only slave here and she was here for other purposes.

The small sandstorm seemed to have blown itself out and the sun was at full strength again, beating down on everything. Rissa looked around to get a good look at this place that her master had chosen for such an important meeting.

To their right was a stone building with columns holding up a wraparound roof and an archway leading in. That was probably the well her master had spoken about because the other intact structure looked like a storage building. Large pieces of stone lay about the area as far as Rissa could see to the left and right. She tilted her head to look at the looming facade. It had obviously been a huge edifice but now it was a crumbling ruin. You couldn't tell what it had been. It looked like it had been sheared off, but the doorway still retained runes above its arch, and she could feel power here.

This was supposed to be a dragon shrine, the home of one of the ancient magical creatures. They had once been plentiful and lived alongside humans and the other ancient race that were now known as

Dune-ers, though rarely seen in their natural form except by their servants. Then a war happened. The whys were lost to time. But many dragons died. Those that survived withdrew and humans became the dominate race in the aftermath as the Dune-ers withdrew as well.

She knew her master had picked this place because this desert was No-Mans-Land, claimed only by the Dune-ers who rarely interfered in human affairs. And what her master had planned was something that he didn't want interfered with.

Her master and one of his men came over to them as the last tent went up. The A-framed tents were spaced to one side between the well and the storage building, leaving a section open for the group her master was expecting. Her master's man grabbed her ward's arm and dragged him away toward the tents while her master held up a hand to halt her from following. "You will have him ready by evening meal day after tomorrow," he told her in a harsh voice.

She gave a half bow in acknowledgment, then hurried after her ward. Her plan would have to be implemented tonight then. The men would party tonight, thinking it safe, but her master would want his men cold sober for the meeting day so he would regulate the ale tomorrow.

So tonight, it was.

I

Rissa carefully slit the back of the tent with the sleeping guard's knife. Of course, his sleep wasn't natural; Rissa had drugged his ale earlier when she had brought him his meal. He would be sleeping for about two hours which would give her and Jors more than enough time to get to the shrine. She glanced over at the teenager.

Jors was typical of his people, the Akiran; snow white hair and blue eyed with a lean build whereas she was typical of the old race; ash blond, green eyed, and stout. Their so called 'master' was typical of his people, the Denea, dark of eyes and hair with muscular bulk, and arrogant to the extreme. She had been a slave for over fifteen years with this master and she had been resigned to being his slave until she had overheard what he had planned for Jors.

The young Akiran had been acquired two months ago and Rissa had been given the care of him, on top of her other duties of course. It had taken their 'master' until now to set up this meet and luckily for her and Jors it was at this shrine. The rumors about this place made it the best chance for escape.

No one really knew who built it. Though it was rumored this place had once been a palace of some long-ago Dun-er king and been destroyed in the dragon war, leaving only the ruined shrine. The shrine itself seemed to be built around an oasis and had two outbuildings, one of which housed a well while the other was completely empty. Visitors set their tents in the area before and between the three buildings. What she had learned was that rumor had it to be the sanctuary of one of the surviving dragons who slept beneath the building itself and only allowed his servants entrance to the enclosed oasis, though the well was for anyone who needed it. The rumors also said that if one went before the servants of the shrine and dedicated your life to the dragon you would be protected and cared for. No man would be your 'master' again.

"Are you okay?" Jors whispered, breaking into her thoughts.

"Fine. You ready?"

"Whenever you are."

Rissa grabbed his hand and pulled him out behind her as they slipped out the slit, making for the next tent back.

The fires were in front of the tents thankfully, giving them darkness behind. Tonight, the men were drinking as they felt safe here at the shrine with the rock-shewn desert all around and two guards on duty. Luckily those guards were looking out. The only tricky part would be getting from the last tent to the entrance of the shrine without the fires revealing them to any still sober and awake.

They slipped along like shadows behind the tents until they came to the one directly in front of the shrine. It was over a hundred yards to the entrance, and light and shadows moved everywhere along that path. There were only five men hanging around the fires and they all seem to be drunk.

"Remember don't look back, just keep running." Rissa told Jors.

"I ain't leaving you alone."

"I should be right behind you."

"You better be."

She gave him a grim smile, then glanced around the small tent to the fires. The men were still facing away. "Whenever you're ready."

He tightened his grip on her hand, and off he went, pulling her along. Neither heard anything behind them as they raced to the entrance. They slammed into the wall that was just inside the entrance and stopped, breathing hard. Jors tugged on her as he moved to the left and entered the shrine proper.

The chamber spread out before them. A line of black stone divided the slate floor widthwise wall to wall with two alters, one on either side of the line but staggered a bit so they were not opposite each other. The altars were carved of the same black stone with a oblong pedestal supporting a rectangular top. Halfway along that top a plain stone sword hilt protruded. On the opposite wall behind the floor line there was an archway that allowed a glimpse of the oasis with rooms on both sides of the arch. There were crystal squares of light spread along the stone walls, lighting the shrine with an even glow.

Dragon magic, no doubt or left over from before the dragon wars.

An old woman of the old race in a linen dress entered the shrine from the archway and stared at them. "Well?" she asked in the silence.

"We wish to become servants to the dragon." Rissa said as she stepped forward.

"Do you?" the woman raised an eyebrow as she moved further inside the shrine.

"Yes." They both nodded.

"Do you know what that entails?"

"Anything is better than what we left." Jors met the woman's eyes.

The old woman looked at them, her eyes intense, then she nodded. "Alright. Come to the first altar."

Rissa and Jors moved to the outer altar and looked towards the old woman to see a ball of light in her cupped hands. They watched as the old woman moved to the other alter and stared into the ball of light before suddenly throwing it at Rissa.

Startled, Rissa immediately threw up her right hand to block it from her face and it vanished just as it touched her skin. Pain shot up Rissa's arm and she looked at her hand, seeing a brand on her palm.

A small dragon with its tail curled around himself was burned into her skin.

As she stared at the branded rune on her hand,

she heard Jors gasp in pain and knew he was now branded too.

"You are now the dragon's servants." The old woman paused as they both looked at her. "You may enter the inner shrine now."

As they stepped over the black line, Rissa felt something pass over her. "What was that?"

"Your protection." The old woman smiled. "Anyone who isn't a servant tries to step across the line and they die. They shoot an arrow or dart, and it stops at the line. The shield goes all the way around the oasis, and it can't be broken. At least as long as the dragon lives."

"They just fall over dead?" Rissa raised an eyebrow.

"They become a pile of ash, actually."

"That what all this dirt is over the outer stone floor?"

"Yes." The old woman laughed. "I get tired of sweeping so I just leave it be. Isn't hurting anything."

"You the only servant here?"

"Was. Now you two are the servants here." The old woman paused. "Alright. Here's how it is. The room on the left side of the archway is the sleeping area with a privy attached while the room on the right is a library. Don't worry about not being able to read something because that's a gift you get becoming a servant; You'll be able to read anything in the library. There are nut and fruit trees in the oasis as well as a spring and a lagoon for drinking and eating, although meat and bread will appear on the inner altar at both midday and sunset to keep you healthy. As to duties, well, servants await the commands of their dragon."

"What does that mean?" Jors asked.

"You may spend your life going about daily living here or the dragon may speak to you and have you do something that he wishes done. The dragon may sleep physically but that does not mean that he is not aware of what is going on around him."

"I plan to remain here the rest of my life, so it doesn't matter to me." Rissa said. "But Jors is young."

"You are both now the dragon's," the old woman told them. "Your lives are now in his claws."

"As I said, anything's better than what we came from." Jors shrugged.

"Excellent. Anything else you want to know before I leave?"

"Leave? "

"Yes, I've waited here long enough for another servant to take over." The old woman stepped over the line and headed towards the main entrance.

"Wait. You can't just leave us here. And you definitely don't want to go outside."

"I'm not going outside, and I'm no longer needed here."She paused in front of the mirror that was on the wall that blocked the straight access from the main entrance. Her hand touched the mirror, and it became another doorway. "I'm tired, and as I said I've waited long enough."

"How long have you been here?"

"One hundred and twenty-three years. Good luck." The old woman laughed and stepped into the doorway which then turned back into a mirror.

"She was joking, wasn't she?" Jors asked, looking at Rissa who was still staring at the mirror.

"I don't know." She shook herself and then looked around. "How about we look at the sleeping area and the library? They'll be missing us soon."

"Do you think they'll come in here before morning?"

"They'll think we made a run for it so they'll look in the desert first."

"We wouldn't make it far without water."

"Slaves are stupid, you know." Rissa gave him a side look. Their master repeated that enough.

"Right."

Rissa headed towards the archway and the rooms at the back of the inner shrine with Jors just behind her. The rooms didn't seem very big, but then the shrine hadn't either so you never knew. She took a step into the sleeping area and looked around.

An open doorway to the right lead into a privy, a tiled privy, so it was probably kept clean by 'magic', water or dragon powered. The dragon no doubt took care of it, one way or the other.

There were bunk beds on the other three walls with long, thin windows at just below the roof level on the back wall to let in air. In the center of the room there was a row of four beds and a large trunk. Glancing into the privy, Rissa noticed an open closet with towels and some sort of clothing as well as the necessary and a bathing area.

"This is definitely better than what we came from." Jors said from over her shoulder before moving back.

"That's for sure." Slaves usually had to make do

with a bucket of water unless they were slaves to the rich. "Let's see what the library looks like."

Jors led the way to the library and they both stood staring just inside the door. Books lined all three walls in front of them from ceiling to floor, and there were waist high bookshelves on either side of the door. To the left there was a long table with chairs while to the right were couches and pillows. On the waist high bookshelf to the right was a large book with writing materials, and Rissa glanced at it to find it a logbook of some sort.

"Much better than what we came from," Rissa agreed with satisfaction as she looked over to Jors. "I think I'm going to enjoy being here."

"Definitely." Jors was staring at the books with wondering eyes. "Even my father's library didn't have this many books."

They both heard a bell as if someone had rung for a servant.

"I'm guessing someone entered the shrine." Jors looked over at Rissa. "Should we go see?"

Before she could answer a different bell rang. Rissa moved to the door and looked out toward the altar. "No one's there now. I think we should go to sleep and see what happens in the morning."

"I am tired." Jors looks at the books again, then turns to Rissa. "I feel like I'm dreaming."

"If we wake here, then we are here." She felt that way too. This place was paradise compared to what she had lived the last fifteen years of her life.

"True. I wonder if bedding is in that trunk."

"Even if there isn't it doesn't matter. I could sleep on rock." And had.

"Well, let's go." Jors moved past her and headed towards the sleeping room's door. "Morning will come soon enough."

Rissa followed him into the sleeping room to see him open the trunk. She took the linen covering he handed her and moved to one of the four beds near the trunk. Throwing the covering on the bed, she flopped down on the mattress and looked over to see Jors collapse on another. As soon as they were settled the room darkened to twilight, and Rissa sighed tiredly. "Goodnight, Jors."

"Goodnight."

Listening to his breathing deepening, Rissa let her thoughts relax and slid into sleep herself.

Tomorrow was time enough to worry.

II

Light awoke her the next morning. Her rest had been dreamless for a change.

She glanced over, then shot up when she noticed the bed next to hers was empty, fear shot through her. But she relaxed when Jors came through the door with some fruit in his hands a second later. "Jors."

"You wouldn't believe what's growing out there!" Jors tossed her a fruit. "There's a pair of knives on the altar with belts. I decided to wait for you before touching them."

"Smart." She bit into her fruit and savored the tart taste before devouring the fruit. Gava was a fruit for the rich and she hadn't tasted it since she was a child at the annual festival that her village used to have. Her mind went straight to what they would probably be facing today as she finished the last of the Gava fruit. She knew their old master was going to be visiting them today, especially after not finding any sign of them in the desert. The shrine would be the only place they could be.

"You think he'll come today?" Jors asked as if reading her mind.

"Yes. Let's go look at the knives." She led the way out of the sleeping quarters and into the main temple. There were indeed two belt knives on the inner altar. Picking one up, she slid the knife out and looked at it.

It was actually more of a hunting knife or a small dagger by its size. The hilt was a claw clutching a ball of crystal at one end and the blade coming out the other. Its belt and sheathe were made of fine leather with silver trim while the blade itself was made of a metal that Rissa had never seen before.

"Can we take them?"

"I think they're for us so yes." Rissa buckled the belt around her waist and settled the blade on her right hip. She could use a knife with either hand so it didn't matter which side it was settled. "Need any help?"

"No." Jors pulled the other belt from the altar and wrapped it around his waist. "These will come in handy with some of the fruit I saw in the oasis. I found a machete on the back wall too."

"StarFruit?" She knew Jors loved the round hard-shelled fruit.

"Yes. And something that looks like Keri but on a bush."

"We'll have to try them some morning." That

hourglass-shaped fruit was her favorite.

Before she could say more, the bell sounded and five men entered the shrine. They were typical Denea, dark and bulky with muscles. Rissa tensed and touched Jors arm. "Jors."

Jors looked at the men for a moment, then took a step back as the men moved towards them.

Rissa took a step forward and crossed her arms over her chest, glaring at the men. She was not going to be afraid of these men. Death was preferable to going back to slavery under their last master.

The men stopped a few feet from the outer alter. Besides their last master, there were his second in command, and three of his best fighters. Their last master took a step forward and spoke. "You shouldn't have run away. Come along now."

"We are going nowhere with you." Rissa met his dark eyes for the first time since she had been enslaved by this man. "You should leave this place before the General arrives and finds you empty handed. He doesn't take disappointment well."

"Don't make this worse for you, Rissa. Just come along and I'll handle the punishment myself."

Jors snorted. "Like that's any better. We are staying here."

"Come here now! I will not ask again."

"You're not asking now," Rissa pointed out, not moving. "As he said we are staying here."

Their last master gestured to his men, and his second in command Nori nodded to the other three. With a return nod, the men moved forward, heading towards Jors and Rissa. However, as soon as the man in front laid a foot on the line in the floor, there was a flare and he vanished, leaving only ashes on the floor. The other two men stopped, then stepped back away from the line. One of the men pulled out a knife and threw it, but it stopped mid-air at the line, falling to the floor. Both men looked back to Nori who gestured them back.

"As I said it'd be best if you leave before the General arrives."

"He will not be put off. He will have the boy." Their last master told her. "He has a Gifted One with him and this 'trick' won't stop him. It would be in your best interest to come with us."

"It's your best interest, you're worried about." Rissa replied to his speech. "You would see a fortune if you turn over Jors to the General and his people as well as a marker you could call in later."

"I will not be used as a bargaining chip by anyone." Jors shook his head. "My father is dead, and I want nothing to do with my past life."

"Doesn't matter what you want, boy," their last master said. "You will do what you are told."

"We are not your slaves anymore, Kori," Rissa told him, calling him the name the General knew him by. He had several names he was known by but none were his real name, though she knew it. She knew many of his 'secrets' because she had been one of his 'trusted' slaves and with him for so long. "Take your people and go before the General gets here or face the consequences."

"You seem pretty confident for someone who is outnumbered."

"You saw what happened to your man." She

gestured to the ashes. "This place is protected and so are we."

A small bag appeared on the outer altar near the Denea. Kori's second in command moved to the alter and picked up the bag which tinkled. The man opened the bag and poured some of the contents onto his other hand. Gold coins lay there, shiny and new. Rissa was sure the bag didn't contain what they would have gotten from the General, but it was more than they had before coming here.

"Take it and go." The deep-voiced words echoed through the temple, and obvious did not come from Rissa or Jors whose lips had not moved.

Nori returned the coins to the bag and moved close to Kori so they could whisper to each other. After a few seconds Nori stepped back and Kori looked at Rissa.

"The General will not be thwarted by these tricks or the offer of gold."

Rissa merely shrugged and watched all the men leave.

"He's right, you know."

Jors sounded defeated and when she looked at him his shoulders were slumped. She moved closer and gripped his chin, raising his head until their eyes met. "We are protected here. Remember we're the dragon's servants. Do you really think a hoarding creature would let go any of its belongings?"

"I hear you," He made an effort to smile.

"Good." She let go of his chin and gestured toward the archway. "I haven't seen the oasis yet so why don't we explore that a bit?"

"Okay."

They both turned and headed outside, stopping just without the opening to stare.

Around them the trees were tall and leafy and what they could see of the sky had an odd shimmer to it. Everything had a green tint to it as the light was filtered through a moving green canopy and the ground was covered in different grasses with two gravel paths leading away from where they were standing. It looked more like a forest than a desert oasis.

Upon closer inspection, Rissa noticed that all the trees were either nut or fruit trees and the bushes were berry or what indeed looked like Keri.

Looking behind her she noticed a machete and a fishing spear hanging beside the archway on the right. "Did you see a pond or anything like that?"

"I didn't go farther than the Gava trees." Jors paused. "But I did notice that."

Rissa looked to the left where he was pointing and saw a small fountain. The dragon's head was extended out of the temple wall and the water ran from its mouth to a small basin below. Two plain metal cups were hanging from its fangs.

It was eerily silent.

She moved to the fountain and took one of the cups. After filling it, she took an experimental sip. The water was surprisingly cool and crisp with a slight tang to it. She drank the rest, then re-hung the cup before turning toward the rest of the oasis.

Before she could say or do anything else, the bell sounded and Jors looked at her.

"I doubt it's Kori," she told him. "But he might

have left a man behind with a message for the General."

Both headed into the shrine to indeed find one of Kori's men there. Rissa recognized him as the guard from Jors' tent. He was carrying a bedroll and a pack, so he was obviously staying.

"Kori must have been very angry with you." As she spoke the man settled down against a side wall with a good view of the rest of the shrine. "You realize that he left you here to suffer the unkind mercy of the General."

The man glared at her but didn't speak.

"General Conn doesn't have any mercy." Jors looked at Rissa. "Do you really think we'll be safe here? The General is ruthless."

"The dragon will protect us," she reassured him.

"This time tomorrow you'll be in the General's hands," the guard growled.

"I think not." Rissa shook her head. "But I know for certain you'll be dead by his hand."

The man glared at her again.

"I'm going to look through that ledger in the library," Jors suddenly announced.

"I think that's a very good idea." Rissa watched Jors disappear into the library before looking at the guard. "Were you any other kind of man, I would feel sorry for you. But like Kori you are the worst of your people and you deserve everything you're going to receive from the General."

The man continued to glare at her but she just turned and followed Jors into the library. She found him seated at the table with the ledger in front of him.

"The other books under this one are ledgers too," he told her.

She moved to the bookcase and pulled out a couple, flipping through them. "Differing hands and long stretches of dates."

"This one begins in a man's hand." He tapped the book in front of him. "It seems he was here for over two hundred years before the writing changes."

"Even my people don't live that long after they reach maturity." Rissa looked at him with surprise. She carefully returned the older ledgers, then pulled out the first one. "You catch up with what our predecessor did and I'll look up the beginning."

Jors nodded as she joined him at the table.

Both soon became absorbed in their respective reading and only when a bell rang did they glance up. This bell was different than the other ; this one sounded more like a dinner bell.

They both got up and headed into the main shrine. On the inner altar was a covered tray and two mugs.

Rissa went and picked it up, barely glancing at the guard. She carried it back into the library with Jors at her heels. They could both smell the roasted meat and Rissa lifted the cover to reveal two plates of bread stuffed with juicy meat. Each took a plate and mug, which they discovered had milk in it, and sat back at the table.

Hunger drove them until the food was gone, then they each relaxed in their chair as they sipped the milk.

"I could get used to this," Jors said.

"So could I," she agreed. Slaves usually subsided

off of scraps and leftovers from meals that servants had first choice of. Many a night she had went hungry.

"Did you find anything interesting?" He nodded toward her ledger.

"The first servant was terse." She paused as she took a sip of milk. "It seems she was a Dune-er."

Dune-ers were dark-skinned humanoid desert dwellers and rarely seen. Those that live far from the desert thought them legend, but Rissa had seen one who did trade with some of Kori's men. Not all of Kori's men were bad, just most of them.

"That would make sense," Jors said.

"The beginning of the ledger covers the first fifty years, according to the date on the last page before the writing changes. What I find interesting is that the shrine and the two outbuildings were already here when she stumbled upon them during a sandstorm. She mentions a servant being here but there's no ledgers before this one."

"Well, the shrine does look like it had been a part of a larger building. Maybe the ones before didn't chronicle or the other books were in the part that got destroyed. Maybe these are what was saved."

"True enough." Rissa nodded. "Fingers of stone do dot the sands surrounding this part of the shrine as if there had been more here. So perhaps the rumors are true and this was once a compound."

"Anything else of interest?"

"A few stories of lost travelers but nothing exciting. You?"

"It seems our predecessor had been something of an Oracle." He tapped the book. "According to this ledger, some desperate people wishing fortune would show up and seek the dragon's favor. Many a greedy man was either turned away or fried."

"That would go with the other rumors I heard." She stood and gathered their mugs onto the tray before picking it up and taking it back out to the alter. Ignoring the guard, she returned to the library to find Jors reading again.

Sitting back down, she too returned to reading, losing herself in true dragon tales.

III

The room was brightening around her but Rissa didn't stir from her bed.

She and Jors had spent the rest of yesterday looking through the ledgers, only venturing out to retrieve the tray of meat and milk that appeared at sundown on the inner altar like the old woman had said. The guard had ignored them both and after a brief glance at him they had returned the favor.

According to the number of ledgers under the open one, this shrine had been here at least two thousand years. The differing hands in half the books suggested that each servant lived for hundreds of years each. While the old race lived longer than the others that was still staggering and made the last servant's words and action seem ominous to Rissa.

Jors sat up, swinging his feet to the floor, and Rissa pushed those thoughts aside. It had no bearing on their life right now.

"Morning," they muttered at each other.

"You want Gava again?" Jors asked as he stood and stretched.

"Yeah." She rolled out of the bed and did her own stretching as he headed out.

The General was due sometime today as the main meet had been set for this evening. There was enough room between the shrine's three buildings for two small groups to camp. Kori had only brought half his covey of warriors; The others had stayed at the main camp situated at the beginnings of the desert. No doubt the General would do the same.

Jors returned with two Gava fruit and handed one to her before biting into the other.

Silence reined as they ate. Every bit of the Gava fruit was eatable, even the seeds, and they didn't let any of it go to waste. It was still a novel experience.

"When was the meet set?" His voice was low and soft and as a result she could barely hear him.

"The initial meet was midday meal." She paused. "But I wasn't to have you ready until night meal."

He nodded, then straightened up his bedding.

Rissa smoothed out her own bedding, then gestured toward the doorway. "You want to continue looking through the ledgers?"

"We need to make our own entry soon,." he told her as they strapped on their knives. "We shouldn't neglect that part of our job."

"True enough." Her knife settled, she led the way out. Once in the main shrine, she glanced over and saw the guard camped out in the corner before returning her attention to Jors. "Do you want to do that or do you prefer me to?"

"I want to." He paused as they entered the library. "Writing is not a usual slave trait."

"I was not always a slave."

"The master mentioned he had you a long time." He set the present ledger and the writing materials on the table. "And the other slaves said the same."

"Kori and I were both twenty when he 'acquired' me. He raided my village on my coming-of-age day and I got to 'celebrate' it with all of his men."

"Rissa…"

"It was a long time ago." She made a dismissive gesture. "Anyway I got beat-up pretty badly but he liked my spunk or more likely the idea of beating it out of me so he kept me. That was over fifteen years ago."

"If you were trouble why'd he keep you or even make you one of his trusted slaves?"

"My village was in Drakland."

Jors stared at her. And well he should since Drakland was now known as the Deadlands and had been virtually closed off for the last fifteen years. Many of those who entered never returned and those who did were tight lipped about their journey.

Some of the Denea clans had gathered together and raided Drakland fifteen years ago, jealous of their prosperity. Unfortunate for some of the raiders one of the towns attacked had been protected by one of the few remaining dragons. The magic said dragon let loose chased the raiders and even the inhabitants from the land. So the land lay empty and ripe. The Denea,and others, still coveted its lush land.

If you could get past the dragon's curse.

"He thought you might be his way back into the lands one day?"

"Yes." Rissa gave a nod. After all it had been her village that the dragon had protected. But she had been dying and weakened. Thus the Denea had been able to pass through her wards and attack. She had used blood-magic to seal the lands. And only blood-magic could unseal it. Specific blood at that.

"Hmm." He settled at the table and took up the pen. "You think I should put our backgrounds in?"

"If you want to." She shrugged. "I don't think there's a set way for these ledgers."

He hummed again and began writing while she moved to the other ledgers and pulled out the first one again. She laid it on the table and settled down to read next to him.

The dragon had actually appeared in human form to the first servant. From what Rissa had heard that was rare; most dragons only showed themselves in their true form the few times they were seen. No doubt to impress.

Dragons were rare nowadays. There used to be thousands but there had been a war among them eons ago and now there were only a hundred known to exist. Perhaps there were more asleep in hidden shrines but rumors only spoke of the known shrines. This ledger spoke in bits about the war and of the aftermath as well as a bit of Dune-er history. It seemed the dragon had been living here since this place had been built centuries before the War by the Dune-ers. According to the ledger, the Dune-ers had once been an advanced society but after the War those that were left took up a nomadic way of life. This shrine being all that was left of a vast complex and the Dune-ers being the only occasional visitors for centuries after the War.

She flipped to the last page she had read yesterday and took up where she had stopped. There was lots to go through yet in this book.

What seemed like only minutes later, the lunch bell rang and Rissa looked up from the ledger. "I'll get the tray," she told Jors as she stood.

He nodded and sat back in the chair.

Rissa headed into the main area and moved to the inner alter. But before she could retrieve the tray, five men entered the shrine and the entry bell sounded.

Three of the Akiran men were dressed in the leathers of common soldiers and another man wore a hooded robe but it was the last Akiran man that caught Rissa's attention. Besides the soldier leathers the older man wore a metal breast plate with a coat of arms.

She had only seen the General once and that in passing, but she knew this was him. The salute the guard gave the man re-enforced this. She remained by the alter and watched.

"Why is Kori not here?" The General demanded of Kori's man. "Where is my merchandise?"

"He had something come up," the guard said. "As to your merchandise…"

"I'm not merchandise," Jors said as he stepped out of the library and joined Rissa.

The General stepped toward them but the robed man moved to block him.

"He just saved your life," Rissa said as the General raised his fist. "We are protected."

General Conn lowered his fist. "Retrieve the boy," he told the robed man.

Without a word the robed man turned and seemed to flow across the floor to the stone line. He reached out a hand which stopped against the barrier.

There was no flash.

Taking a step back the robed man used both hands to lower his hood to reveal a young Akiran man who couldn't have been much older than Jors. "The dragon is alive & awake."

Everyone looked at him for a moment, then the General scowled. "I need the boy."

"I want nothing to do with my past life," Jors declared.

"You will do as you're told," the General growled. "I'm destined to rule Akira itself."

"Then you don't need my father's little fiefdom."

"Crais is a steppingstone." General Conn looked at the robed one. "Get me the boy."

"My dragon was dead and her remaining magic was weak," he told the General. "So you took me easily. You kept me because of my Gift of Foresight. That same Gift tells me this will not end well if we persist."

"I will tear down this shrine stone by stone if I have to. That boy belongs to me."

"I belong to no man," Jors told him. "We are servants of the dragon."

"I'm not making an idle threat; I will tear this place down."

"I think not." Rissa shook her head. This place had survived a magical dragon war so what could a human do to it? Not to mention the dragon itself. "As your Gifted One said…"

"Juls. I'm called Juls."

"As Juls has said that will not turn out well for you." No one liked their home disturbed so she suspected the dragon would respond accordingly. Like the one who had guarded her village. Rissa picked up the tray and moved towards the library. "Now if you'll excuse us we're going to eat our lunch."

"I'm not done with you yet."

"Too bad. We are." She ignored his growled, "Come back here", and kept walking.

Jors followed her silently until they were in the library. "Do you think he'd really do that? Try to tear down the shrine?"

"I don't know." She shrugged before she set the tray on the table and sat down. "But surely the dragon wouldn't let that happen."

"I hope not." He accepted the milk and sandwich before he settled at the table. "For a minute there I thought the barrier had failed."

"Him being a servant would explain why he's not ash. But you saw he still couldn't cross the line." He made her uneasy. There was something not right about Juls.

"You don't think he was just playing with us

all?"

"No." She shook her head. "He's genuinely afraid of the General." That she was sure of.

"I don't blame him."

They both began eating and didn't speak again until they were finished. Gathering the dishes Rissa put them on the tray and stood.

"No use putting it off." She picked up the tray and headed toward the doorway.

The General, Juls, and two of his men were still in the main area. They all looked up and watched her return the tray to the alter. When it vanished, the two soldiers made protection signs and the General scowled at them, causing them to back away a step.

"You can save yourself the trouble and just hand the boy over now." The General looked at Rissa. "Though my men would welcome the chance to know you better."

"That stopped being a threat years ago," Rissa told him. Fifteen to be exact. Kori and his clan had not been gentle those years ago, but she was the one who had to live with the consequences. "Now I would advise you to replenish your water supply and leave this place, preferably by noon tomorrow. If you do you might be able to catch up with Kori."

"And if we don't take your advice?"

Rissa looked steadily at the General. She was not going to show him any fear or uncertainty. "You won't like the consequences."

"I have destroyed many things to get where I am and to get what I want." General Conn moved closer to the barrier. "Nothing will get in the way of my destiny."

Remaining silent, Rissa stared at him, unimpressed. After everything she had gone through with Kori and his men, death or anything else at the General's hands did not scare her. Besides she was sure the dragon wouldn't take kindly to the Akiran General's actions.

"Why can you not pass the barrier?" Conn asked Juls. "I need the boy."

"I can't by-pass the wards."

"Wards?"

"If it was just the barrier I could enter as you have seen me do before since I am branded." Juls paused as he laid his hand against the barrier. "However, with the dragon being alive there are wards added; one of which prevents any but his own servants entrance."

"So if we were to hunt him down…"

"Do not even joke about that, milord General."Juls withdrew his hand and looked at Conn. "The dragon could kill *us* before your men even found his resting place."

"Why are you helping him?" Jors burst out from the library doorway.

"Dragons belong to the past." Rissa heard bitterness in his words. "We must make our way in the now human-ruled world."

"Your dragon died, leaving you at man's mercy. Unfortunately for you that man was the General." She pitied him that. "But you helped the General raid other shrines where the dragon was dead as well."

"There are many. " Juls met her eyes. "As I have said the dragons belong to the past"

"Jazeer"

The word echoed through the shrine.

Conn and his men looked around but Juls and Rissa just stared at each other.

"You are faithless," Rissa said quietly. "You do not deserve to be a servant."

"Drac Su, Drac Na Su"

Even as the words echoed, Juls hissed and fell to his knees, clutching his right wrist. He stared at his palm and started shaking his head in denial. "No, no…"

"What…" The General took a step toward Juls who jerked his head up.

"No!" Juls threw out his hand to the barrier and vanished in a flash, leaving behind a pile of ash.

"Seems he would rather be dead than at your 'mercy'," Rissa told the General.

"I don't understand. He was a servant."

"Was being the main word. The dragon had taken away that Gift." She paused. "Drac Su, Drac Na Su. What a dragon does, a dragon can undo."

"I will tear this shrine to the ground!" The General moved to the outer alter and slammed his fist down on its surface. "I will stake you here after my men have taken their pleasure…"

"They will get no pleasure from me. You think Kori was a kind master?" She snorted. There was nothing the General could do that Kori hadn't. "This is getting us nowhere. By noon on the third day you need to be gone."

She turned and slipped past Jors into the library. With a sigh she flopped on one of the couches and moments later Jors joined her.

"You okay?" he asked her.

"I will be, especially when they're gone."

"What do you think the dragon will do?"

"I don't know." She closed her eyes. "I'd dry up the well if I could."

"Yeah, they'd have to leave at some point then." Jors agreed. "Rissa, what that Gifted One did..."

"Would you go back to Kori?" she interrupted, looking at him.

After everything she'd been through she had almost given up, then Jors had come along. He had renewed her will. To be a slave again, especially Kori's, no. Death would be preferable. She would never be any man's slave again.

"No." There was a firmness to his voice that she recognized. He was just as committed as she.

"Then enough said."

Jors nodded, then looked over at the books on the table. "Shall we go back to reading?"

"I'm not in the mood." She paused. "I'd like to walk in the oasis, but I don't want to be harassed by the General." She just wanted him gone.

"Maybe if we just ignore them?"

"Doubt that would work. I'll just lie here for a bit. You can read if you want." She pulled her legs up and settled on the couch. Maybe a nap would give her some perspective.

Jors went over to the table and Rissa closed her eyes. She felt a light touch as if someone laid a hand on her head, and she felt a warmth flow through her. Her thoughts grew hazy and her mind slid into a dreamless sleep.

IV

The touch of Jors' hand on her shoulder jerked her awake. She sat up and swung her legs down. "Jors."

"I've been hearing strange noises from the shrine." He glanced over to the doorway, then looked back at her. "Do you think the General is keeping his word about tearing down the shrine?"

"The dragon won't let him," she reassured him and herself. The dragon wouldn't allow his home to be torn down. His hoard no doubt resided here. "Let's go see what the noises are about."

Jors nodded and followed her to the door after she got up. He stayed behind her, even as they stepped into the main part of the shrine.

It looked like the General's men were building some sort of rolling ram. The ram part itself was covered in metal but the rest of the small contraption was wood as were what looked like wheels. Where they had gotten the materials to make it Rissa didn't know. And she had never seen a ram with an arrow-like head before.

"A Felkin," Jors murmured.

That she had heard of. It was a siege weapon of the Akiran. The ramming part shot out and hit full force of whatever air pressure it was set at. Rare was the material that could withstand the constant hammering it produced. But why the arrow shape?

Before she could ask Jors, the General caught sight of them. "This will take care of that barrier." He patted the ram. "It will fail under the continuing pressure."

The warmth from earlier was still with her, keeping her relaxed, and no fear overwhelmed her. She didn't think the ram would have the effect that the General thought it would. The barrier was magic and dragon magic at that. Plus the ram wasn't iron. Non-Landers didn't know of that caveat. So she believed the General would be disappointed. If the dragon itself didn't just smite the thing."You are mistaken."

"Nothing can withstand the Felkin."

"Your arrogance and greed will be your downfall."

Conn just laughed.

His men moved the Felkin close to the shield and at the General's nod started it to its work. The arrow head slammed into the invisible barrier, making sparks fly but nothing else seemed to happen each time it hit.

After watching it for a few minutes, the General looked at his men. "Watch it. If it fails before I return come get me."

The men nodded.

With one last glance at the Felkin Conn headed toward the entrance. Before he got there Kori's man called to him and the General turned toward him. "I'll get to you soon enough," he told Kori's man, then left the shrine.

Snickering was heard from the General's men.

Kori's man glared at Rissa and Jors.

"I told you," Rissa said. "Kori is beyond his reach right now, but you are not."

He growled, then returned to his huddle by the wall. If he had tried to leave they all knew the General's men would have stopped him.

The tray appeared on the alter just then though no bell rang. Rissa picked it up and she and Jors retired to the library. They took their time eating, enjoying having meat that wasn't raw or burnt and milk that wasn't sour or spoilt. This was paradise to them.

When they were done, Rissa gathered the dishes on the tray. "I'm going to go for that walk. Do you want to come?"

Jors looked at the open ledger beside him, then shook his head. "I think I'll finish this up. There's only a little bit to go."

"Alright. I should only be gone a candlelight," she told him.

Giving her a nod, he slid the ledger closer and began to read.

Rissa picked up the tray and went back into the

main part of the shrine. Conn was back but she ignored them all as she put the tray back on the alter. When it disappeared Rissa turned her attention to the others.

The General and two of his men were standing in front of Kori's man. Conn was holding Kori's man against the wall with a hand on his chest. Kori's man was pleading that much was clear though Rissa couldn't hear the words just his voice. They were speaking too low and were just too far away from where she stood.

Suddenly Kori's man screamed and jerked.

Conn removed his hand and the man dropped to the floor.

She had warned him but like all Denea he had been arrogant. Well, like most men, she corrected, no matter their race.

After kicking the corpse, the General turned and saw her. He said something to the two men, then moved closer to the outer alter. "That will be your fate once my men have a turn with you."

"As I told you before that stopped being a threat a long time ago." She turned and headed for the oasis archway. "Make sure your men take out the trash," she said over her shoulder before stepping into the oasis.

It was a little darker out here as it was evening but she could see quite well. She decided to take the right-hand path and began to walk. Flora was all around her within seconds and the light a darker green. The air was fresh and the beginnings of the headache she had been getting faded away as she continued around the slightly curving path. A small lagoon about the half the size of the outer shrine with a rocky waterfall on the far side appeared to her right where the path curved more to the left. Behind and under the waterfall she saw part of the stone that enclosed the oasis. It was the same dark stone that marked the temple floor.

A head popped out of the water and she stopped as more of the creature emerged.

It was a winged dragon!

Wings flared a bit as he climbed out of the lagoon, then settled on his back .He looked like what one would expect a winged dragon to look like, only in miniature. About the size of a large house cat, he was four-legged, but the front legs were more arm like with clawed hands and his long tail ended in a triangular spike. His eyes were like emeralds, shinning out of his glimmering gold scales.

Rissa caught her breath. He was beautiful.

Varun

The name appeared in her mind gently as though he was afraid he would scare her. She inclined her head to him in acknowledgment.

A whiff of smoke came out of the dragon's nose as he stared at her for a moment before moving toward her. There was something purposeful to his movements.

Rissa stood her ground though she had felt a bit of unease at the unblinking stare.

Your hand

She bent and held out her hand to him.

He darted out his head and nipped her index finger, drawing blood.

Rissa jerked it away and stuck it into her mouth at the sharp pain. Amusement and satisfaction radiated from the dragon and Rissa tried to frown at him around her finger.

Be at ease, Keeper. I am not laughing at you. Just your reaction.

"Why'd you bite me?"

The dragon didn't answer as he turned and slipped back into the lagoon.

"Hey!" She took a step forward but the dragon disappeared under the water before she could say anything else. When he didn't re-emerge after a few minutes she huffed in frustration, then whirled and resumed walking on the path. No use waiting. She had a feeling he had completed what he wanted to do and would not be returning anytime soon. Though why he had wanted to bite her she didn't understand.

Seeing the small lagoon though had brought to mind the bath. Perhaps she would use it tonight. There had been towels and clothing. She wish she could wash away the past as easily as she would the dirt. But a bath would be a start as well as new clothing. Emerging herself in this new life literally. Get rid of the trappings of her old life.

The back of the shrine appeared ahead and she quickened her pace. She and Jors could bathe before they went to bed tonight and take a long soak as they did so. It's not as if they hadn't bathed together before. Though this would be the first in an actual bath. And slaves didn't have the luxury to be body shy or conscious.

In the shrine the Felkin was still pounding away

on the barrier but it didn't seem to be weakening any. The general's men glanced at her, then returned their attention to the Felkin as she moved toward the library. Jors was sitting at the table reading a ledger when she entered and she stopped just inside.

"What do you think about using that bath?" she asked as he looked up. "I think it's time to shed these rags and check out the clothing in that closet."

Excitement lit the boy's eyes as he hastily closed the ledger and got up. He hurriedly returned the ledger to its place before joining her by the doorway. "Let's do it!"

She messed his hair with a smile, then led the way to the sleeping area, both of them ignoring the Felkin and the General's men. As soon as they entered the sleeping area both started stripping off their clothing. They made it to the privy area before they were completely naked. Convenient hooks just inside the bathing area took their belt knives.

Jors paused and looked at the scars covering Rissa's mid-section. "Rissa…" His voice trembled.

"You saw them before."

"Not all of them."

"It happened a long time ago, Jors. Now let's get that bath." Her voice was fake-cheerful. She refused to think about the past. It was time to look forward.

He nodded and they both moved toward the pool.

The closet and a bench were on the rear wall. Steps led down around the outside of the pool into the faintly steaming water. Tile lined both the twenty-foot square chamber and the pool. There was no piping or drain to be seen. This chamber had to be as controlled and operated by dragon magic as the contained privy was.

Rissa spied two bottles in a recess on the top step and entered the warm water near them. Jors just jumped in, aiming for the middle of the pool where he could see it was deep. While Jors tread water in the pool's center, Rissa sat on a lower step so that the water came just up to her shoulders. This much water was unheard of amongst slaves. Several slaves had to use a single bucket if their masters were generous. If not spit and maybe an oil rag.

The bottles turned out to be lathering soap. Rissa used it heavily. She had years of filth to remove, both literally and figuratively. Her hair and body felt refreshed after she was done. She settled back on the step and watched Jors play in the water.

He looked and acted younger than his fifteen years. No doubt both a defense mechanism and the result of his captivity. Children were not punished as severely as adults whether they were slaves or just regular children, but child slaves tended to be smaller due to lack of proper feeding. Jors had been five when his father had been killed and he had been sold into slavery by the murderer. His mother had given herself to that same murderer to insure Jors was given that chance to live. He hadn't understood it then but wisdom had come with the years.

When Kori had bought the boy, Jors had been prickly and defiant and Kori made him her responsibility. She had been whipped quite regularly at first for Jors' escapades but she had never said a word to stop him. After the whippings she'd still take care of him as if nothing had happened. He'd stopped his escapades after a while and Rissa found that she had developed a liking for the boy. Then she had overheard Kori and one of the General's men talking about Jors' fate as a bargaining chip. Thus their escape and present circumstances.

Jors grabbed a bottle and did a hasty wash before settling on the step above hers.

Rissa almost fell asleep as she relaxed against the pool. She stretched, then climbed out of the water and headed toward the closet.

Inside were robes, tunics, and pants as well as large towels on the shelf above the clothing. They were all the same emerald color as the dragon's eyes.

Grabbing a towel, she dried herself off before she dropped the towel to the floor. She picked a tunic and pants that looked her size and slipped them on. They fit comfortably. She moved away from the closet and headed for her belt.

Jors grabbed her towel from the floor and dried himself with it, then dropped it back to the floor. He too chose a tunic and pants to wear. His hand rubbed the material and he looked at Rissa. "It's soft."

"It's infused with spider silk," she told him as he slipped his clothing on. A yawn erupted and she rubbed her face tiredly. "I'm for bed."

"Me too." He glanced toward the direction of the main shrine area.

"They won't get through the shield," she told

him, reassuringly. "The dragon will protect us."

Jors didn't look convinced but he followed her into the sleeping area and curled up on his bed.

Rissa hung their belts on the little headboards, then settled on her own bed as the light dimmed. Just as she slid into sleep she realized she hadn't told Jors about the little dragon. Tomorrow. Tomorrow she would tell him.

V

Breakfast consisted of Gava again.

Rissa would never get tired of that. It reminded her of her childhood. A good memory. She could hear the Felkin hammering away, though just barely, but ignored it as she finished her Gava. Every bit of the fruit was edible and the juice wasn't sticky like a lot of fruits. She licked her fingers of what little juice there was, then stood and buckled on her belt knife.

Time to start the day.

Jors swiped his hands down his tunic before standing himself. He slipped on his belt knife, then raised an eyebrow at her.

She shook her head at him but he just grinned at her.

After a stop in the necessary, they strode out of

the room and into the main shrine. The General and two of his men were near the Felkin but Rissa and Jors ignored the Akiran as the two of them continued on into the library. Rissa grabbed one of the old ledger books, then settled on a couch while Jors took the current ledger to the table and sat down.

"Tell me what it says," Jors said as he opened his ledger. "While I write."

"It won't disturb you?"

"No."

Rissa leaned back into the arm corner and drew her legs up to rest the book against her thighs. She opened it and scanned the page. "This one seems to be when the servant was an Oracle and many people came for their fortunes. Caravans also came through with regularity from Akira to the Denea Kaydee Market."

"So after the rise of the Great Kings and before their assassination when the Accords actually meant something."

"I see you paid attention when your tutor taught you ancient history." She looked over at him.

"Father and a few of the other Lords were trying to raise Akira back to that ideal. The General wants to be the one on the center seat, but Father was against that. He told me a great leader studied the past as well as the present and ruled fairly with this knowledge and he didn't think the General was such a man."

"Obviously." She paused. "You remember everything your father said to you?"

"Yes. I may have been young but I worshiped

him."

"As I did my father." Rissa looked back down at the ledger as she pushed away the past. No use thinking about something that she couldn't change and she had no room for pity—self-directed or otherwise. "This day the caravan was late..." She began to read.

A gong sounded from the main shrine, interrupting her.

Both of their eyes went to the doorway, then Rissa set the ledger aside and stood while Jors laid the pen down and got out of the chair. The gong sounded again, louder as if demanding their attention, and they headed to the door. A third gong came as they entered the main shrine.

Five of the General's men dragged two bodies toward the shield, then threw them down in front of it, just far enough away not to accidentally touch that deadly force. One of his men kicked the bodies until a moan came, showing that they were not dead. At least not yet. She was sure the General didn't plan to let them live for long.

Rissa and Jors moved to the inner altar and stood behind it, facing the men.

The General entered the shrine. In his one hand was the small bag that had held the gold the dragon had given Kori for her and Jors. He was tossing it up and down as he strolled toward his men.

She turned her attention back to the two bodies lying on the floor. Their features were swollen from the beatings they had taken but she did recognize Kori and his man Nori. So the General's men had caught up with them. They mustn't have gotten far, despite their head start.

Stopping by his men, the General looked over at her and Jors. "They told me a very interesting story."

Rissa didn't say anything. She just rested her right hand on the stone sword hilt of the inner altar and stared at Conn. Why she had the urge to touch the altar she didn't know but she did know she didn't want to engage the General about which story Kori and Nori had told him. The two Denea after all knew her secrets, just as she knew theirs.

The General smirked at her, then looked down at the two Denea and kicked one of them. "Rabble will bare their pitiful souls if they think it will spare their worthless lives."

"Judgment shall be rendered." The words rang through the shrine even as another gong sounded.

Jerking his head up, the General looked around, seeking the author of that voice.

There was a fluttering of wings and Rissa glanced up to see the small dragon from the lagoon soaring in a circle above her and Jors. It circled again, then landed on the altar, facing the General's group.

The General and the dragon stared at each other.

Rissa felt another presence in her mind. It was the dragon. She recognized the touch from before. Her apprehension and bit of fear left her.

"This is the dragon?" Conn's voice held derision.

"Don't let his appearance fool you," Rissa said. "dragons are formidable."

The General gave a contemptuous laugh. "dragons are nothing."

Silence suddenly reigned as the Felkin fell silent. One of the General's men immediately went over to it and messed with it for a moment, then looked back at the General. "It won't start back up and I can't find anything wrong with it."

Varun showed his teeth in a dragon grin.

"Is that supposed to intimidate me?"

Smoke swirled around his head as the dragon chuffed, obviously laughing at the General.

The General's mouth tightened and he glared harder at the dragon.

"You should have left when my Keeper told you to." The words rolled through the shrine.

"I will not leave without the boy. He is mine."

"No, he is mine."

Rissa tightened her lips. Jors wasn't a thing, he was a person. The presence sent a feeling of comfort and agreement and she calmed a bit.

"I have dismantled other shrines," the General told the three facing him from the altar. "And destroyed whole cities. You will not stop me from fulfilling my destiny."

"The faithless one gave you a key but it doesn't fit every lock."

"That's not the only key I have." Conn tossed the coin bag to one of his men, then pulled a small pouch from his waist and juggled it a bit.

Rissa made a sound of apprehension . She recognized the pouch as Kori's and knew what was inside. Kori had searched for years for a way to counteract the dragon's curse of Drakland, and that pouch contained one of the trinkets he had found. While it would not undo the curse, it was something powerful and could not inconceivably cause problems for the dragon.

At her gasp a smirk had lifted the General's lips. "As I said they bared their grimy souls to me," he told her. He opened the pouch and poured the content onto his one hand. "It was made by an Adept."

Adepts had been the magic users of the Old Race. They had fought alongside their chosen dragon companions during the War. None survived. And magic in the old race seemed to have died with them.

The General held up the necklace by its chain for all to see.

It was a double-sided pentagram. Inside that pentacle was a silver rune. Rissa had recognized it as a character from the dragon language as soon as the seller had shown it to her master. So had Kori. He had bought it right away. That he had given it up was indeed telling.

The medallion and chain were iron. Hence possible trouble for the dragon. Or rather his magic. Cold iron disrupted magic, but spells could be laid while it was hot and being formed. After it was cooled, the iron hid the magic signature but the spell was solid.

"Did you know that there was only three races originally?"

Conn frowned at this nonsequitur, this seemingly unrelated question from the dragon.

"We dragons, the Dune-ers, and the ones you call the Old Race. You Akiran and the Denea were created by the Adepts as slaves using blood-magic.

Which is why the basis of your languages are so similar to the ancient tongue. It was the disagreement about that slavery—and a timely revolt—which led to the war and the creation of baubles like what you hold."

"Bauble?" The General scoffed. "It's more than that."

"Adepts were masters of blood-magic; however, dragon magic is different."

The General frowned again.

Rissa knew that dragons could do blood-magic but indeed their main source of magic was not that. But iron still interfered with the effectiveness of magic, dragon or blood born. However whatever spell was on the necklace may not work within the dragon's sphere of magical influence.

"You obviously think it will work against the shield. How are you going to test that?" The dragon showed its teeth again in a grin.

The General slipped the medallion over his head and settled it over his chest plate before tucking the pouch at his waist. But he did not advance toward the shield.

Another chuff of laughter came from the dragon. His eyes glowed for a second, then dropped to the two Denea lying on the floor.

Kori and Nori had regained consciousness and were struggling to sit up. After a few tries they managed to prop themselves up with their trembling arms.

"Kaj Kori and Nai Nori, you sit in Judgment." The dragon clapped its front clawed hands together twice and suddenly both men were on their knees, kneeling. "Kaj Kori, for what your Clans did fifteen years ago you all were justly punished by the protective dragoness. However, your personal crimes are why you are in Judgment now."

Kori raised his eyes and chin defiantly.

"Death would be merciful for you," the dragon continued. "It would be more fitting to let you live with the knowledge that you had a key to Drakland within your grasp all these years."

Rissa stared at the dragon in apprehension. Was he going to tell them the secret?

The General had a speculative expression on his face.

Nori just looked confused.

Kori's face went blank for a second, then he swore.

"Blood-magic sealed the land and blood-magic would free it." The dragon grinned toothily again. "You had a key, but instead of treating her like gold, you abused her."

"A key?" The General raised an eyebrow.

"Five of us had our Ascension that day," Rissa told him. "The Ceremony included blood-magic, readily available to the dragoness for her to use to seal the land. Any one of us can be a key."

"You should have told me!" Kori growled.

"Would you have stopped what you were doing to me if I had?" she flung back. "Your men had already had their fill. Had you killed me I would have been happy!"

Kori growled again.

"Which brings us to your true punishment." The dragon drew a glowing rune in the air in front of him with a claw. "You shall have no product or pleasure from your loin."

Kori screamed as the rune burned itself into his chest. He slumped, then fell over onto the floor, unconscious.

Nori glanced at Kori, then stared at the dragon, his eyes fearful.

"Take him and go. Steal a horse if you wish, but be gone from my shrine."

Glancing at the men around him, Nori didn't move.

"They won't stop you. Nor the men outside. Go!"

Nori got up and dragged Kori to his feet before slinging Kori's arm across his shoulders and heading for the entrance.

The General glared at his men who indeed didn't move.

"I have frozen them. They can see and hear but no other movement."

Conn deliberately took a step forward.

Varun gave another huff of laughter.

"Why did you let Nori go without punishment?" the General demanded.

It was Rissa who answered him, not the dragon. "He shall receive it either when Kori awakes or when the reality of the curse first shows. Would you not kill the witness to your shame?"

"Nori is a loyal man. To have that loyalty betrayed..." The dragon paused. "My Keeper has given you a deadline for leaving. By noon tomorrow be gone." He launched himself into the air and flew out the back archway, disappearing into the oasis.

VI

"Get the Felkin working." The General glared at his men before looking at Rissa. "I shall have you both. I will rule Drakland and Akira."

Rissa glanced over to where his men surrounded the still silent Felkin, then stepped back from the altar, allowing her hand to drop from the stone sword hilt. "You will rule nothing."

"I have sent for the rest of my men and supplies. They will be here in two days."

"Then they will share your fate if you do not leave by noon tomorrow."

"I do not fear your dragon."

"You should." She grabbed Jors arm and dragged him toward the library. Once inside the room, she let him go, then went to a couch and collapsed on it. "Gods," she cursed as she ran a hand over her face.

"Rissa..."

It was too much. Her emotions were in so much turmoil that she didn't know what she felt. Kori, she knew, would have much more preferred death to what the dragon had done to him. But it was just deserts for him to suffer what he made so many experience.

Keeper

The thought was accompanied by a mental tug.

She got up from the couch and went back to the archway. "I'll be back," she said over her shoulder before walking into the main shrine again. Ignoring the men still around the Felkin and the General yelling at them, she headed for the oasis entrance, then, once she went through, kept walking until she was at the lagoon.

The dragon was waiting for her on one of the flat rocks on the lagoon's edge.

Keeper

Rissa frowned at him as she sat on a rock near him.

His death would not have balanced the scales.

"I know." And she did. But a part of her still wanted him dead. However another part of her got a sick pleasure thinking of what he would now suffer. She was conflicted as she knew she shouldn't be feeling pleasure at another's suffering even his. But she couldn't stop herself from savoring the thought of what Kori would endure.

The dragon cocked his head as he continued to stare at her.

Rissa dropped her eyes and picked at imaginary lint on her pants.

There is no reason to feel guilt or shame at your emotions.

Her eyes flashed back up in startlement.

Why the surprise? You can feel my presence in your mind.

"Suspecting something is one thing, but getting confirmation is another," she told the dragon. "Why didn't you judge the General? Is it because of the talisman?"

You gave him a grace period. He is an advocate until then and as such I can't judge him unless his conduct here becomes unacceptable.

"Trying to destroy your temple and kidnap us is acceptable behavior?"

I expect rude conduct from angry humans.

Rissa could tell that the dragon didn't think of either act as more than a child's tantrum. "But the talisman, it's iron."

So it is.

The dragon seemed amused, though by what Rissa didn't understand. She knew cold iron was inimical to dragons and magic alike. It could kill or incapacitate him. So why was he not worried?

"Rissa."

She started at the sound of her name and turned her head to see Jors coming toward her with the food tray. "Jors."

The teenager set the tray on her rock, then grabbed his sandwich and mug before sitting on another rock facing the dragon and her. He put down the mug, then took a bite of the sandwich, watching both of them.

Eat, the dragon told her when she didn't take up either one.

Rissa picked up her sandwich and started to eat, realizing how hungry she suddenly was. Her anxieties had twisted her stomach.

Do not worry. Everything will be resolved tomorrow.

She raised an eyebrow.

You will see

The dragon was amused again. She watched as it slid into the lagoon and disappeared again under the water, then returned her attention to her food. Worry was indeed a useless thing as she had learned during the last fifteen years, though that didn't stop her from doing so anyway.

Both she and Jors finished their meal and set the mugs on the tray which vanished as soon as they removed their hands. Jors returned to his rock and Rissa turned so she was looking at him. They sat silently for a while.

"You were not shocked or surprised when the dragon came," Jors said.

"He had revealed himself to me the other day," she told him. "He came out of the lagoon, bit me, then disappeared back into the water. I had planned to tell you about it today."

"Bit you?" He threw a concerned look toward the water.

"He nipped my finger." She showed him her hand so he could see it was fine. "Maybe it's a sign of affection."

"Still." Jors frowned.

She knew what he really wanted to talk about, but she wasn't ready to broach that yet and was grateful he wasn't pushing it. "I will tell you the whole story of my past someday, but not now."

"I understand," he told her.

And she knew that he did. His life was not as personally tragic as hers but tragedy did played a huge part. That she knew more about his history than he did about hers was accidental and because he had been new to Kori's bevy. Kori's 'kinks' had been well known to his men and slaves, especially the female enslaved as they were marked by them.

Jors slid off the rock and stood. "Should we finish what we had started this morning?"

Rissa got to her feet as well. Her emotions were not settled but she was calmer and she knew worrying didn't help anything. So she took a deep breath and let it out slowly, then gave herself a shake before she started to walk back toward the shrine.

With a skip, Jors caught up to her and walked by her side.

It didn't take them long to get there at the brisk pace Rissa had set. They stepped into the shrine and paused to allow their eyes to adjust to the dimmer light.

The Felkin still wasn't working. Two of the General's men were messing with it while the General himself was standing by the mirrored wall talking to three more of his men.

Rissa and Jors continued on into the library. Jors sat back down at the table while Rissa resumed her seat on the couch and picked up the ledger she had set aside. She settled the book against her thighs, then looked at Jors who was fingering the quill pen.

Without looking up, he told her, "I'm afraid."

"I know." She understood. The dragon was powerful, but so was the General. Men like the General usually got their own way, sometimes even through powerful opposition. No matter what one tells oneself fear always makes one doubt. And their life experiences have shown that happy outcomes rarely happen in the real world.

"What if..." He stopped as though he couldn't go on.

"Jors, look at me." She met his eyes when he did. "One way or another you will not be the General's pawn."

Jors stared into her eyes for a moment, then nodded before returning his attention to the ledger in front of him on the table. "What happened since the caravan was late?" he asked, changing the subject, as he dipped the pen.

"An Akiran lord was suppose to be traveling with it to the shrine for a Telling. She says the lateness was a foreboding of what she had to impart to him."

"The Telling was a negative one and she already knew it?" He had started to write in the ledger but paused to glance at her.

"Yes."

"Hmm." He went back to writing. "Perhaps fate had already intervened then."

"She writes that it had. The whole caravan disappeared. It seems the lord was on an errand for the Great Kings and his disappearance was contributed to a conspiracy according to this note left along the margin."

"Does she write what the Telling was?"

"No." Rissa flipped the pages. "But she does write that the world outside the shrine will change and not for the better. Then there is just stuff about the day-to-day things she does. I haven't gotten too far in this book. Each chronicler writes differently. Some just the highlights, others everything."

"I noticed that myself. I think some of them were lonely."

"Or meticulous."

"Well, I don't plan to write that way." He closed the ink bottle and cleaned the pen before looking at her. "The dragon was talking to you, wasn't he, when we were at the lagoon?"

"Yes." Her forehead wrinkled and she frowned. "You didn't hear him?"

"No." He shook his head.

"How did you know where I was, then?"

"I felt a tugging."

"Maybe it's harder for him to project to two." The wrinkles in her forehead smoothed out as she thought of that.

"Perhaps. But he called you his Keeper."

She frowned again and her brow wrinkled once more as she recalled that the dragon had, several times in fact. Those that served a dragon were called servants, so the legends and rumors said. And no man could command them, any more than he could the dragon. Everything she had read in the ledgers confirmed that

But no where had she seen or heard mention of a

Keeper.

Tomorrow will reveal all.

The word carried promise and reassurance that everything was as it should be. She accepted it as such and pushed away the worry. Anyway worrying did no good. Didn't change anything outside her control. "Maybe that's what the head servant is called."

"Perhaps." But he didn't seem convinced.

Rissa returned her attention to the ledger propped against her thighs. "This servant was only here another year. It abruptly ends, then another hand writes in it two years later."

"The shrine was unattended for two years?" Jors sounded shocked.

"If I'm reading the dates right the absence was during the time of the assassinations of the Great Kings and part of the aftermath. Turbulent times. Everyone fighting each other. Besides from what I've read in other books the shrine's been unattended a few times."

"Not the ones I've read."

"You've only read the recent ones. Which I want to hear. At least about the one before us."

"Her name was Ianira and she was an Oracle too." He looked down at the ledger and flipped back a few pages. "She had a vision of us a few days before we showed up. Not a true Telling, just a vision."

"I wondered at her attitude."

A loud cladder came from the main shrine. And with a look at each other, they stood and went to see what had transpired.

VII

The Felkin lay in a heap on the floor in front of the shield with the General standing over it. He wasn't, she noticed, wearing his breast plate, but the medallion was in full view. And his men were staring at the heap in shock.

Rissa began to laugh and Jors joined her.

Conn looked at her and scowled. "Imagine your shield doing this," he growled as they continued to laugh. "You won't think it funny then."

"Perhaps not," she said as she and Jors stopped laughing and straightened. "But are you so sure it will be the shield that fails?"

The General scowled at her some more, then turned on his heel and headed for the entrance. "Fix it!" he growled over his shoulder at his men.

His men looked at each other, then at the pile on

the floor, but didn't move closer.

"Fix it or death will be the least of your concern," the general growled before disappearing around the entrance.

One of the men knelt and picked up a piece of wood. It turned to powder at his touch. He glanced toward the entrance, then back down at his powdery hand before looking up at his companions. With a grunt of "wood" one of them headed for the door, dragging another man with him.

The evening tray appeared on the altar and Rissa retrieved it before leading Jors back into the library. They sat at the table and ate the meal without conversation. Once again as they set their mugs on the tray and withdrew their hands it vanished, causing them to start a bit.

"I guess he's watching us," Jors said.

"This is his home." It made sense to her that the dragon would know what was going on within his shrine but she too hadn't realized he was watching that closely. She pushed that thought away and went back to what they had been discussing before they had heard the cladder. "You said the servant before us was an Oracle and had a vision of us?"

"Yes. Unlike the Oracle you spoke of, Ianira wrote her visions and Tellings down. She said such was to be shared ever if only in a book. There wasn't many visitors, seekers."

"What did she see?"

"A young woman of the Old Race during a Coming-of-Age Ceremony screaming as Denea raiders swept in, then a little Akiran boy kneeling beside a dead man with another man standing over them with a drawn sword."

Rissa closed her eyes as emotions threatened to overwhelm her and pushed those emotions back in their boxes. She had learned to put her emotions in mental boxes and present an emotionless facade. Kori was not a kind master. He was a true sadist and so enjoyed causing pain, whether physically or emotionally. Therefore, she had learned to control at least her outward expressions. And time had dulled much. But sometimes the past overwhelmed her despite all that.

"She says she had a feeling of expectation after the vision so she knew she was to meet them. According to the entries after that one, the feeling grew stronger every day. And she was glad. I think she was lonely. The dragon rarely spoke to her and visitors were sparse and very far between." He paused. "I'm glad you're here."

Her eyes opened and she looked at him. He too had suffered from Kori but he did not hide away most of his feelings. Jors openly showed his anger and defiance, no matter the consequences of that. However he had never shown much of other feelings he may have had, though he had relaxed his guard around her. This was only the second time he had admitted anything beside mutual hatred of Kori, his situation, and of course his fears about his uncertain future. He had told her she had his respect after the third beating she had taken for him without turning around and taking it out on him. Now he was saying he enjoyed her company in what was sort of a back-handed compliment.

He closed the ledger on the table, then stood and

picked it up. "I don't plan to be meticulous." He stumbled over the big word a bit, showing he hadn't spoken it before. "But I plan to write every day."

She could see he was a bit embarrassed about showing his feelings by his refusal to meet her eyes so she allowed him the change of subject. "It's your choice as you're the chronicler."

Giving her a nod, he then turned and moved to put the ledger back on it stand. He settled it carefully, then joined her on the couch. "Rumors say that Drakland had been the only vestige left of the time before the assassinations of the Great Kings, that it was a flourishing civilization of the Old Race."

"It was." She closed the book resting against her thighs and set it aside. "But we were naive and arrogant too. We took things for granted. The Denea raid and the successive route and sealing by the dragoness showed us that. I wouldn't doubt that our numbers have fallen as well."

"I heard many people talk about what a boon it would be if someone could unlock Drakland from the Curse. Even some of the slaves dreamed of being the one who would be able to do so."

"The land may be fallow of people but there is treasure aplenty lying there for the taking. Everything was left behind. The sealing drove the people from the land with only the clothes on their backs and what they could carry in hand. It killed some of the Denea."

"Too bad Kori wasn't one of them."

"If he had been we would have never met and you might even now be in the General's hands."

"How did you know that you were a key? You were obviously in Denea hands when the sealing was done."

"Yes, but we were part of the sealing so we knew as the spell was worked."

"Why did Kori keep you then if he didn't know?"

"Partly because that raid was his first after his manhood test and I was a reminder of both success and failure. And partly because he suspected the sealing was blood-magic work so he wanted a ready source of blood from a former resident. But I suspect mainly because I survived him. Most of his slaves are such."

Jors blinked. "Is that why they're so..." he trailed off.

"Yes." She didn't say anything more about that. "Of course the five I mentioned was just in our village."

Laughter burst out of Jors and Rissa smiled.

When he calmed down, she said, "How else could she seal the whole land?"

"How indeed. Though Old Race blood is known to be potent."

"A remnant of our magical past."

"Now that I think about it all the blood-mages I've seen or heard about have been Denea or Akiran."

"Our Priests could still preform our Coming-of-age and the Earth-Taking Ceremonies but higher magics were beyond them. Oracles showed up every so often. And there are probably still Healers among my people. However we never reached Adept power again and probably never will."

"We keep coming back to depressing subjects. I didn't mean to; I just wanted to know about Drakland."

"I know. But life is full of shadows as we both know all too well." Talking with Jors had actually revealed that she was no longer angry about the past. She was still sad and still felt the pain but the anger had passed. Of course, the punishment the dragon had given Kori had helped a lot. It wouldn't change anything, but it gave her a sense of closure, the feeling she could finally move on. That she could now live.

"Yes."

His voice was sad and Rissa looked at him. He was staring down at his hands that rested in his lap. She realized he was probably still living in the past, and that he probably would as long as men like the General sought him out. He wouldn't be able to move on because others would seek him out to use as a pawn because of who he had been. Until that stopped, the past wouldn't let him go.

"The General will leave one way or the other tomorrow," she told Jors firmly. "Empty handed," she added at his sharp look.

"He sent for his men."

"That won't help him."

Jors dropped his eyes again and began to fidget.

"What did you want to know about Drakland?" she asked. He obviously was still thinking about the General and what would happen tomorrow. She knew he'd have problems sleeping if he didn't get his mind on something else.

"You already dispelled a lot of the rumors. It was

considered a magical place with dragons being common as a faraway unknown land is."

"To Akirans. But the Denea tribes that were our neighbors knew better. That's why they took the chance to raid us. However that didn't turn out like they thought it would. Instead of gaining land and riches, they and everyone else was driven away."

"The rumors say that Drakland was at the height of civilization."

"We were. We had what we called Modern Conveniences. Which contributed to our naivety and arrogance. We thought nothing could touch us, bring us down because of our civilization."

"Crais had some steam-powered factories and solar powered lights that were left over from the time before the Great Kings got assassinated. Father had people working all the time on improving the life of our people."

"We had harnessed the tectonic forces and used it and the sun to power our lands. There were machines to help us in every aspect of our life, farming and industry. We were indeed at the height, the envy of our neighbors. Had they approached our leaders we probably would have helped them at least establish the basics. At least I'd like to think so."

"When do Denea ever ask for anything?" Jors said bitterly. "Of course some Akiran are that way as well."

The sound of a Felkin hammering away came suddenly from the main shrine.

Both of them looked towards the doorway as the sound just as abruptly stopped. It did not return after a few minutes and they both relaxed, turning their attention back toward each other. But before they could say anything a crash came from out in the shrine. They exchanged looks, then stood up and moved to the doorway.

The General was kicking one of his men who was lying a midst what had been the new Felkin. His other four men were standing at attention off to the side, keeping their eyes averted. The man's who the General was kicking hand brushed the shield and he vanished in a flash, causing the General to be off balance and nearly fall.

Rissa and Jors kept quiet, though a smile touched both their faces at the General's near fall, just watching the scene play out before them.

"You Dogs will fix this properly." The General gestured to the mess next to him. "Or you'll be begging for what just happened to Qual. Do you understand me?!"

"Yes, General," the men shouted, their eyes still averted.

The General turned on his heel and stalked away toward the entrance wall.

Once he vanished around the entry, Jors spoke, watching the men gather around the Felkin pile. "Will he really kill them if the Felkin fails to work?"

Rissa nodded.

"But it's not their fault."

"To men like him that doesn't matter. If he doesn't get his way, it's always someone else's fault, someone he can punish, take his frustration out on. I'm sure he sees himself as perfect, the benign ruler who must punish the imperfect sinners. He probably tells everyone he's doing everything for the sake of the people, that they would be better under his rule."

"Do you think he really believes that?"

"No. But that's what he wants everyone else to believe about him. To get them on his side. At least until he does become their ruler."

"He's just one man. His men could easily overpower him."

"They wouldn't even think of that." Rissa shook her head. "To them he's larger than life. He's the boogieman and a god all rolled up into one. I've seen the way they look at him. He must have done something seemingly impossible or has some true fanatics loyal to him that keep the others in line."

The two of them watched the General's men mess around with the Felkin for a moment before Jors yawned.

"Come on. Let's try and get some sleep." Rissa gave him a smile before stepping out into the shrine.

Jors followed her, and they both ignored the men as they moved toward the sleeping area. Once they were inside, they headed into the privy, then as soon as they finished there they almost fell on their beds.

Her emotional and physical fatigue drew Rissa almost immediately into sleep once she was horizontal.

Tomorrow. Tomorrow she could worry. Tonight she was too tired.

VIII

Exhaustion had kept her asleep for a few hours, but dreams had seeped in eventually. Nightmares really, though they didn't stay for long each time. The dragon would appear and she would slip back into deep sleep. But the dreams would return and the sequence would happen again. So she did get some sleep. Just not enough.

Jors seemed to be his normal self. However, his eyes gave him away. He was scared of what today would bring as well.

They finished their breakfast of Gava, then Rissa made a stop in the privy before they stepped out into the main shrine.

A Felkin stood in front of the shield, but it must not be operational as it was not running right now. The General's men looked like they hadn't gotten any sleep last night. They were frantically working over the Felkin so the General must be due anytime.

Jors and her hurried into the library. Neither of them wanted to be there to witness the General's arrival. Jors grabbed a ledger and moved to the table, but Rissa bypassed the ledgers and scanned the spines of some of the other books.

She found a small thin book that just had the word 'dragons' on it and pulled it out before going over to one of the couches and sitting. "Hmm."

"What did you find?"

"A book about dragons. I think it's Dune-er. And for children."

"What's it say?" He turned sideways in the chair to look at her.

"Dragons are the children of Malthe, the God of Fire and Death. They live beneath his shrines. Which it seems the Dune-ers had a lot of as Malthe was their prime deity. There are lots of pictures of the shrines" She flipped through the pictures. "I don't see any of the dragons, just a few statues of them."

"Actual pictures?"

"Yes. This book must have been made before the War. Plus there are trees and grass in these pictures. Which makes sense since this is a dragon shrine."

"True. What else does it say?"

"Dragons have servants to care for the shrine and do their bidding in the World as the dragon themselves guard their Hoard and the shrine's holiest of holy where Malthe's Spark is located."

"Malthe's Spark? What's that?"

Rissa flipped through the last few pages. "It

doesn't say. Guess Dune-er children know what it is."

"See if you can find any other books about dragons or this Malthe's Spark."

She nodded, then got up and went over to one of the bookshelves. After re-shelving the book, she continued her scanning of the spines. She finished scanning one bookshelf, then moved on to the next. The books were not in any order. Perhaps she would fix that.

"Rissa, you need to see this."

The strange tone in his voice made her look up and over at him. He was holding what looked like a small photograph. She straightened and moved to join him at the table. Her eyes widened as she looked at the picture.

It was of a woman dressed in a spidersilk robe with a dragon sitting on her shoulder. However what had surprised her was that the woman looked enough like her to be her sister. And she was an only child. Unlike the Denea and Akiran there was great diversity in the Old Race beyond hair and eye color and for this woman to look that close to Rissa, they had to be related.

"Does it say who she is?"

"It was used as a bookmark." He flipped the photo over and showed her the blank back. "But it must have been taken before the War too. There's grass and a tree in the background."

Rissa took the photo and stared at it. "What was it marking?" she asked absently.

"You know I've been reading backwards from the servant before us." He paused for her nod.

"Well, the second one before her was a scholar of sorts. He was interested in the War's aftermath, mainly how the kingdoms came to be. It was marking the entry with some of his notes about what he called the Charter."

"Charter?"

"He said it was a list of rules for governing the land."

"Laws in other words."

"He says it was more than that. I haven't read it all yet."

She took one last look at the picture, then handed it back to him before going back to the bookshelves. "Keep reading. I'll continue looking for more about dragons."

"Okay." He went back to reading the ledger as she started on the books again where she had stopped.

Rissa doggedly kept looking but it seemed only that children's book was about dragons. She did find a book about Malthe and she sat it down on the floor by her feet as she continued to scan the spines. Her eyes were getting tired from all the squinting and reading.

A gong sounded, startling them both. Two more gongs came in rapid succession.

The two of them looked at each other, then Jors slid out of the chair before they both headed to the doorway. They paused there, then stepped into the main shrine.

Two of the General's men were by the Felkin while the other two were standing behind the General who was glaring at the two by the Felkin.

He transferred his glare to Jors and Rissa as they moved to the inner altar.

"You were to be gone by now," she told him as she and Jors stood behind the altar and faced the others. Her hand moved to rest on the altar's sword hilt and another gong sounded.

He moved forward until he was close to the shield. "Not until I have destroyed this place and you and the boy are in my hands."

The flap of wings announced the arrival of the dragon. He landed on the altar and stared at the General. "The deadline has passed. My Keeper has been generous, but no more." The words rolled through the shrine. "Take your men and leave or face the consequences."

"You do not scare me. I will have the woman and the boy and maybe even your gold."

"And I thought the Denea were arrogant. Your past triumphs do not guarantee you victory. They were against the dead and dying. I am neither. Naois!"

A Dune-er entered the shrine from around the front entrance. At his side was a Ras, a large black scaled doglike creature. The Dune-er himself was black-skinned with silvery eyes and white hair that fell in a braid to his shoulders. He was dressed in skin-tight garments that looked to be made of Ras hides and a hooded slick sand-colored cloak that hung down his back to his ankles. A silver sword hilt peered out over his left shoulder through a slit in the cloak.

The General's men stared for a moment, then ran toward the Dune-er, drawing their swords.

He drew his own sword, but remained where he was as he awaited the men racing toward him.

For the Dune-er to enter through the front something must have happened to the General's outside men. Rissa suspected they were dead. Dune-ers didn't travel alone. They traveled in what they called Bodhi, groupings of at least five. That this one was alone in here meant to her that the others were outside.

One of the General's men fell and did not get back up. The Dune-er was a whirlwind and was holding his own against the three remaining men. Another man fell and did not get up, this time due to the Ras. The Ras began to harass the other two as the Dune-er continued to fight.

With a angry growl the General lunged forward, passing the line with a sizzling sound. Not pausing he drew his sword and kept charging toward the altar.

The dragon took to the air and dodged the sword swing the General made.

Rissa pushed Jors behind her and backed away from the altar. She drew her dagger and kept her eyes on Conn. The man was seething. She could almost feel the hatred and anger coming off of him.

"You shall pay for interfering," he growled at the hovering dragon before turning his attention to Rissa. "Give me the boy."

"No." She moved them both back another step and held her dagger at ready. He lunged forward and swung at her, but she used her dagger to divert his blade. She had watched and been around Kori's men enough that she knew the basics of blade fighting. But she also knew she was no match for a soldier like the General and his men.

"Your dragon can't help you as long as I have this." The General patted the medallion hanging on his chest. "And you are no match for me. Just give me the boy and I'll let you live."

"No," she repeated.

"Then so be it." He darted forward and swung, hooking her dagger, then with a twist of his blade disarmed her. Using his weight he pushed her to the ground, falling with her and landing on top of her.

All the air swooshed out of her and Rissa struggled to breathe as she tried to get out from under the Akiran. The General suddenly stiffened, then his weight rolled off of her and she lay there, gasping for breath.

Above her the General was trying to reach the dagger sticking out of his back near his shoulder. He finally managed it and tossed the dagger to the floor before retrieving his sword. "You shall pay for that, brat," he told Jors who stared at him defiantly.

Rissa clambered to her feet and moved to Jors side.

A triumphant yell had them all looking toward the other fight. The Dune-er had defeated another of the General's men. Now it was one-on-one and it was clear the Dune-er was better than his opponent, even without the Ras' harassment.

"I would take this time to escape if I were you," Rissa told the General.

"I'll be back," he growled before taking her advice. The shield sizzled as he passed and she could tell he was hurting. Next time he would wear his breast plate all the time. It had been a glaring mistake on his part and she knew he would not make it again.

Keeper

There was sorrow in the presence and word.

She looked at the hovering dragon. Varun couldn't have done anything as long as the General wore that medallion, she knew that. She had no hard feelings toward him about that at all.

Keeper

There was still a touch of remorse, but gratefulness was the main feeling.

Another triumphant cry came and they all looked over to see the Dune-er standing over the body of the last of the General's men. The Dune-er wiped his sword off on the dead man's leggings, then sheathed it before turning toward them. He stood there for a moment looking at them, then walked up to the shield.

The dragon landed carefully on Rissa's right shoulder.

"Keeper." The Dune-er bowed to Rissa. "I am Naois Dark. And this is Keir," he added as he laid a hand on the Ras' head.

Rissa knew Dark would be the name of the Bodhi he belonged to as the Dune-ers had two names, the personal and the Bodhi, to differentiate themselves. "I am Rissa and this is Jors."

Naois bowed again, then held out a hand toward her. "Come with me."

Fear reared up, but reassurance came from the dragon and she moved toward the shield.

"I'm not staying here alone," Jors said, following

her.

"You may come as well, Colt," Naois said.
Rissa stopped just short of the shield.
The Dune-er met her eyes steadily.
She took his hand and stepped over the line.

IX

Outside the air was thin and dry, a far cry from the shrine. She and Jors had followed Naois out to the well building, the Raya he called it. They stood under its extended roof and watched the others.

Four Dune-ers were milling about, taking bodies from where they lay to three pyres nearby. Naois stayed by her and Jors' side as the others worked. Another Ras ran about the area as well, though it looked smaller than Keir. It didn't take the Dune-ers long to finish the pyres, even after retrieving the bodies in the shrine. They picked up the unlit torches that had been leaning against the one pyre before heading toward the three of them at the Raya.

The dragon shifted a bit on her shoulder. She

didn't really feel his weight at all, just a slight heaviness as if she was carrying a large book there.

Holding the torches in front of themselves, the Dune-ers came to a stop in front of Rissa. Two of them stepped forward, a man and a woman. The woman had a burn scar across her neck and cheek, but that didn't take away the fact that she looked similar to Naois. Both wore the same garments as Naois but their braided hair fell to the middle of their chests.

"This is my sister Anais and her mate Koa," Naois told her.

Rissa inclined her head to them and they bowed to her.

The other two stepped forward. They too were dress the same as Naois but their hair was braided along the middle of their heads and ended just above the hood of the cloak.

"My cousin Anala and her mate Aza." As he spoke the two Dune-ers bowed.

Rissa inclined her head again. "I am Rissa and this is Jors."

All four bowed again.

The other Ras joined them and Naois said, "And that is Zev."

Anais bowed again then held out her torch. "Malthe Salvis."

With a flash of light, the torch burst into flame. The other Dune-ers lit their torches from hers and with another bow to her, they all headed toward the pyres. As soon as they reached them, the Dune-ers set them a flame, then arranged the torches in a square around the perimeter of the pyres. The fires all flared up into the sky and formed a fiery dragon. It burned for a moment, then with a flash everything disappeared.

The pyres, the torches, and the fiery dragon were gone, with no sign they had existed.

Rissa blinked, then looked at Naois.

"Malthe's Spark," he said as if that was an explanation.

She shook her head. "I don't understand."

He frowned at the dragon who was looking a bit sheepish, well as much as a dragon can.

"And this Keeper bit. I don't understand that either."

"Your dragon is young," he said. "You would say High Priestess."

"Okay." She drew the word out a bit, hoping he'd say more.

"Keepers are the only one allowed in the dragon's lair and the Holiest of Holy where Malthe's Spark resides. They are the caretakers of both. Your dragon really should be telling you this," he added, looking at the dragon sitting on her shoulder.

You weren't ready to hear then.

Rissa had been in a different frame of mind when they had first come.

"Shall we return to the shrine?" Naois asked, offering his hand again.

"Yes." She took his hand and allowed him to draw her along.

"What was this place?" Jors asked as he followed them.

"The palace of our ruler Kaja Dune."

"Is that why you call yourselves Dune-ers?

Children of Dune?"

"Quite right, young colt."

Jors smiled.

Naois allowed Rissa to enter the shrine first, then followed her with Jors behind him. "It will be good to finally have a Keeper here. Too many Sparks have died and the land has suffered."

"Is that why it's a desert?" Jors asked. "We saw pictures from before the War. There were grass and trees."

"Many of Malthe's Sparks died or were destroyed during the War. shrines like this one are all that are left from that time. We withdrew to this land because it was inhospitable to the humans and this had been the heart of our land.."

Rissa and Jors stepped back over the line into the inner shrine area before turning to look at Naois.

"The General destroyed a few shrines in his campaign," Jors told him. "Across Akira."

"We have felt the Sparks die," Naois said. "Evil has spread more after each death."

"Isn't Malthe's a god of death?" Rissa asked.

"There are different types of death." The other Dune-ers entered the shrine and stood behind Naois. "I must speak to the Elders. We cannot allow this to continue."

"They haven't listened before," his sister said.

"Ah, but now we have another Keeper in the palace. And one related to Lessa if I'm any judge."

Anais looked sharply at Rissa.

"Who was Lessa?" Rissa asked Naois.

"The last Keeper here during the War. She kept Malthe's Spark from dying when the dragon was killed and helped that one hatch." Naois pointed to the dragon on her shoulder. "You have her look."

"That picture!" Jors exclaimed.

"We must go," Koa said. "We are already late."

Naois nodded, then bowed to Rissa. "We will take our leave of you."

"What if the General comes back with the rest of his men?" Jors asked. "He sent for them."

"Do not worry about that. His wound will have festered by now. And we will set up a watch. None will travel the sands that we do not see." He bowed again, then turning, led his Bodhi out of the shrine.

The dragon jumped, then glided to the altar. Their noon tray appeared next to him.

They both rushed to the altar and attacked the food. Rissa hadn't known how hungry she was until she had smelled the meat. Jors had obviously felt the same way. Minutes later, they were done and sitting the mugs back on the tray. It vanished and Rissa sighed.

Keeper

Rissa looked at the dragon. There was a tentativeness to the word.

You are not angry.

It was more a statement than a question but she answered it anyway. "No. You were right that I wasn't ready to hear. I was angry and not in a good place."

"You were not the only one," Jors said.

"Naois mentioned a Holiest of Holy." She was tired and wanted to change the subject. "Where is it? I haven't seen another room."

That's because it's below ground.

"Below ground?!" she exclaimed.

"I didn't see any stairs," Jors commented.

Grip the sword hilt, Keeper, on the altar. Then lift up and back.

Rissa moved until she could comfortably reach the stone hilt and wrapped her hand around it as if she was going to draw it out. She pulled as directed.

The hilt slid up a few inches, then laid down flat. Rumbling, the altar began to move forward, causing Rissa to let go and step back. The dragon took to the air and hovered as a large dark cavity was revealed in the floor. A rim of the same stone as the altar surrounded the hole.

As soon as the altar stopped moving, Rissa stepped forward and looked down the revealed opening. A winding stair of stone led down into darkness.

The dragon landed on her shoulder. He sat silently, waiting.

Rissa looked at Jors.

"Go on. I'd already be at the bottom. I'll be in the library." And he turned words into action by heading off toward the library.

She watched him go for a moment, then looked down the hole. The darkness really didn't beckon her.

It is not dark once you are down there.

Taking that as encouragement, she stepped forward and went down the steps. It indeed got lighter as she went until when she reached the bottom it was as light as day.

An archway faced her. There were sparkling runes set around it. They were a welcome and a warning.

She stepped into the small room.

Another archway led off to the right but half of the room was taken up by a large egg-shaped diamond. It was mounted in a stone setting made of the same black stone as the altar. As she got closer she could see there was something in the diamond's center.

A flame. An eye-shaped flame seemed to burn in the center of the diamond.

"Malthe's Spark?" She stopped a hand's breath away from the stone mount.

Yes. The heart of the shrine and the source of our power.

She raised a hand, but hesitated. Encouragement came silently from the dragon in her mind so she touched the diamond.

Warmth raced up her arm into her body. With it came a presence not unlike the dragon's but more encompassing. It swept through her, then suddenly it was gone except for a lingering trace in her mind. Varun's presence was stronger but she could still feel the other and when she mentally touched it, it too became stronger.

Welcome, Keeper

Her hand dropped from the diamond. "What?" she forced out of a tight throat.

Yes, welcome, Keeper.

EPILOGUE

Rissa heard the entrance bell. She looked over at Jors who had been writing at the table as she set aside the book she was reading. Aside from visits from Naois and his bodhi it had been quiet in the month since the General had been here.

"Maybe it's Naois again," Jors said as he stood.

"Well, let's see," she replied as they both headed toward the archway.

It was indeed Naois and his bodhi who were waiting in the shrine. With them was an older Dune-er. His garments were woven as was his cloak which was what Rissa had seen on the Dune-ers that had traded with Kori's man and his sword had a plain hilt.

They all bowed to her, then Naois and the stranger stepped forward. "Keeper, this Nalda. He is an Elder."

"Greetings," Rissa said as she and Jors stood by the altar.

"Keeper." Nalda bowed again. "Did you know that before it was divided up into Kingdoms by the first kings that all this land was called Draksovran?"

Rissa shook her head at his pause.

"The three races lived harmoniously. Until those now called the Old Race grew arrogant. They created the Denea so they would not have to do physical labor and the Akiran for servants, exploiting the Blood-magic the dragons had taught them to use long ago. The Denea grew resentful and the Akiran wanted freedom to pursue other things beside servitude. People chose sides and thus a War began. We and the dragons were caught in the middle. Many of our Keepers were of the Old Race and torn between duty and family. The Adepts were vicious in their zeal. Thus many of the shrines ended like this one."

A flap of wings announced the dragon's arrival. He settled on Rissa's shoulder, facing the Dune-ers.

"Malthe finally took a hand. He stopped the War by smiting the Adepts . The Adepts simply ceased to be and would never be again. This show of power stopped everything. And the five top Generals of the War became kings, dividing the land into kingdoms. We were tired. So we withdrew into this land that no one wanted. It was a reminder of what arrogance can do." He paused. "We have grown complacent, we Dune-ers. The outside world didn't concern us. But it has intruded, bringing with it some realization. We are not truly isolated here. What goes on out there affects us. And Malthe is showing us this."

"While I enjoyed the history lesson," Rissa said. "I still don't understand what that has to do with you coming here."

"It is time we rejoin the world and bring it back to harmony. We are here to ask your blessing and get your guidance in this."

Rissa stared at them. Did they mean what she thought they meant?

"Give us your wisdom as Lessa had given hers to Dune," Nalda told her. "And we will remake this world with it."

Author Note

If you have enjoyed this book, then please leave a review to help other readers to experience the joy. Also, Authors love feedback.

I have an email list. If you wish to join or just want to see what I'm doing go to the web version of my blog at

https://tlriffey.blogspot.com or
https://tinariffey.blogspot.com
The book blog for this series is at
https://dragconicsidereal.blogspot.com

ABOUT THE AUTHOR

Tina Riffey always wanted to be a writer. She started with poetry in grade school and moved to stories by high school. Through a series of moves, she lost those earlier stories, but continued to write down story ideas through the years.

This is the second book in her Fallborn Series. Books in the Fallborn Series are set in different worlds where dragons either are or have been. Book 1, *The Last Dragon Kin*, is available on Amazon and Kindle Unlimited. Check it out.